nickelodeon

P9-BUH-073

FULL SPEED AHEAD!

Illustrated by Omar Hechtenkopf

A GOLDEN BOOK • NEW YORK

© 2015 Viacom International Inc. All rights reserved. Published in the United States by Golden Books, an imprint of Random House Children's Books, a division of Penguin Random House LLC, 1745 Broadway, New York, NY 10019, and in Canada by Random House of Canada, a division of Penguin Random House Ltd., Toronto. Nickelodeon, Blaze and the Monster Machines, and all related titles, logos, and characters are trademarks of Viacom International Inc.

ISBN 978-0-553-52455-0

randomhousekids.com

CRAYONS MANUFACTURED IN CHINA

Book printed in the United States of America

10 9 8 7 6 5 4 3 2

Meet Blaze, the fastest Monster Machine in Axle City!

Axle City is where the Monster Machines live.

© Viacom International Inc.

AJ is Blaze's driver and best friend.

Help Blaze and AJ get to the Monster Dome for the Monster Machine World Championship.

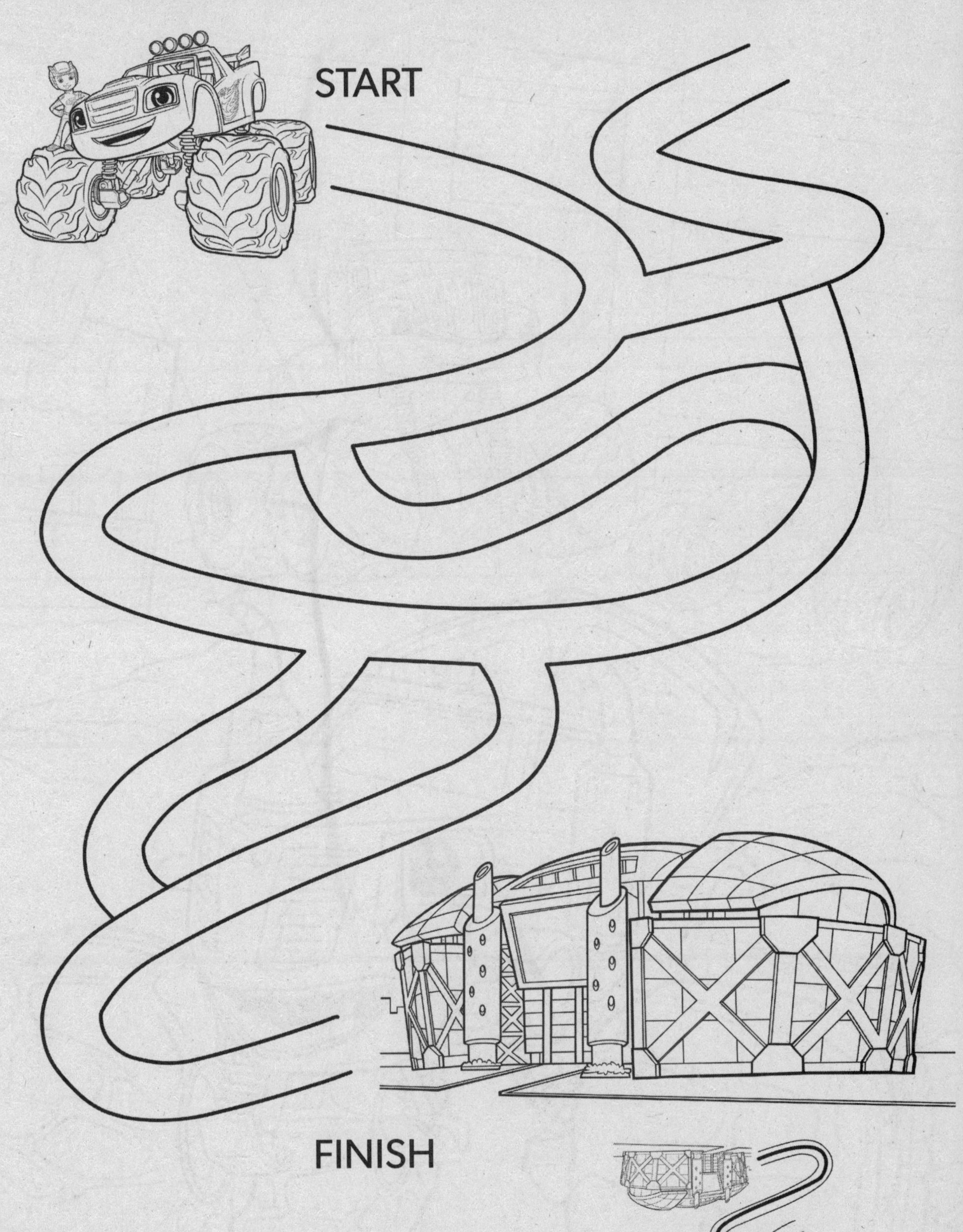

ANSWER:

© Viacom International Inc.

Check out the awesome racetrack!

Blaze and AJ say hello to Gabby the mechanic. She takes them to meet the racers!

© Viacom International Inc.

Darington dazzles with his tricks and stunts.
But he doesn't always stick the landing!

Starla is a hootin', hollerin' cowgirl Monster Machine!

© Viacom International Inc.

Zeg the dinosaur truck loves to smash and bash!

Stripes the tiger truck is always ready for action.

© Viacom International Inc.

Crusher will try any underhanded trick to win.

Crusher's sidekick is a mini monster truck named Pickle.

© Viacom International Inc.

Match each Monster Machine with its close-up.

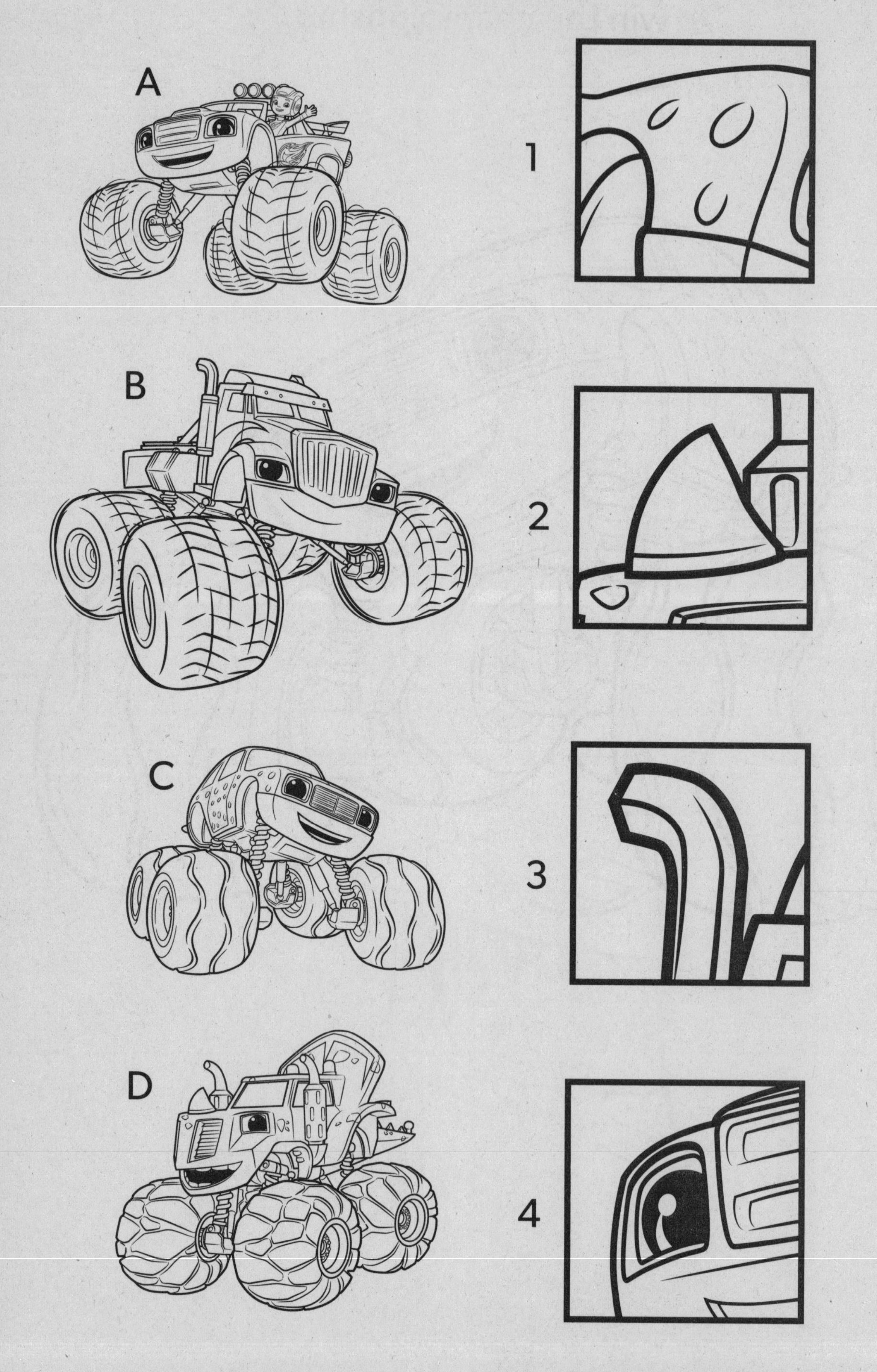

ANSWER: A-4, B-3, C-1, D-2.

Crusher will do anything—even cheat—to win the championship.

© Viacom International Inc.

Crusher's Trouble Bubbles carry the other racers away so he's the only one who can race!

Zoom through the maze to find out where Blaze and AJ's Trouble Bubble is headed.

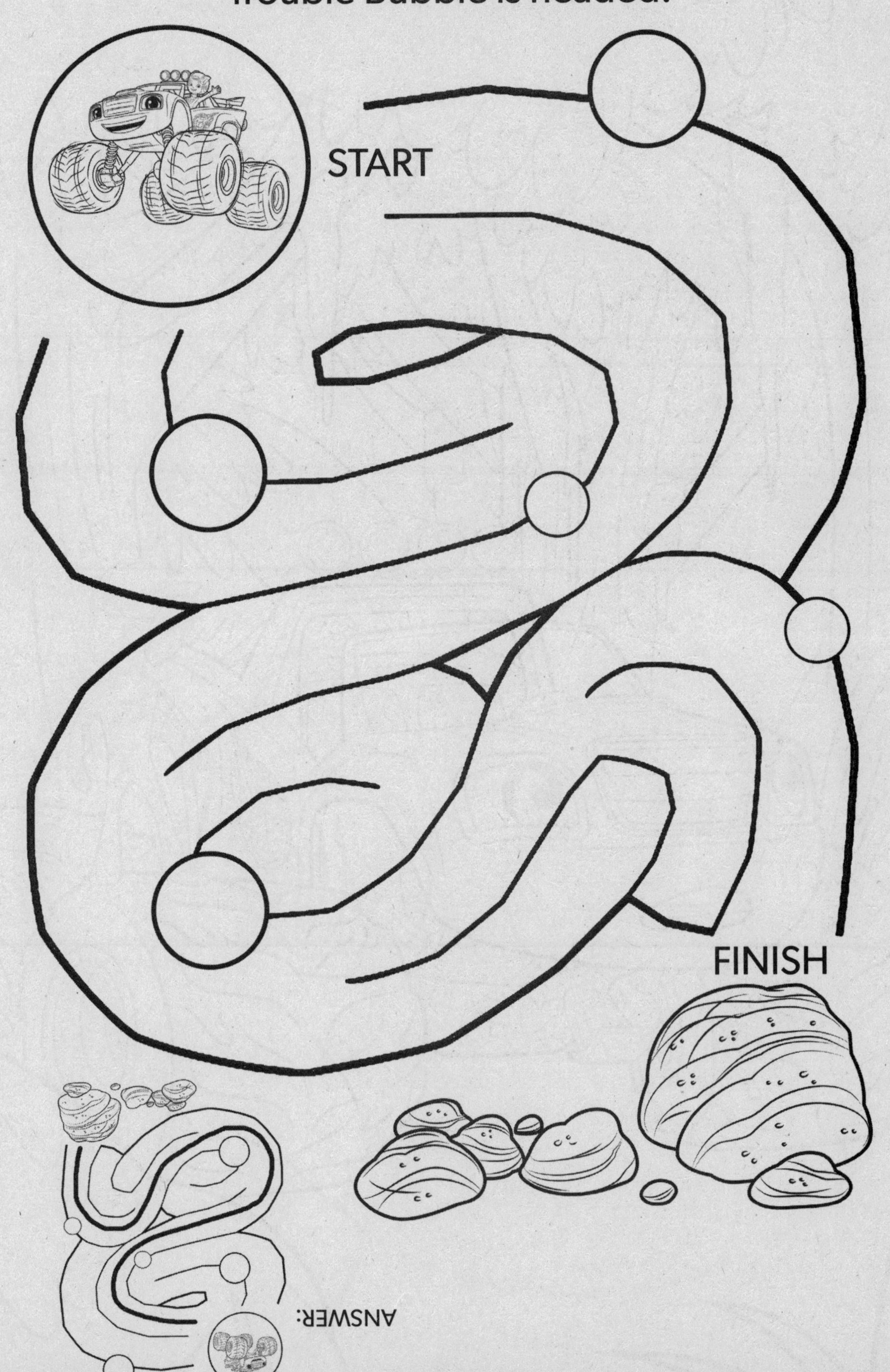

© Viacom International Inc.

Blaze and AJ spot something in the Badlands.

It's Stripes—and he needs help!

© Viacom International Inc.

AJ switches to Visor View.

Which ramp does Blaze use to reach Stripes?

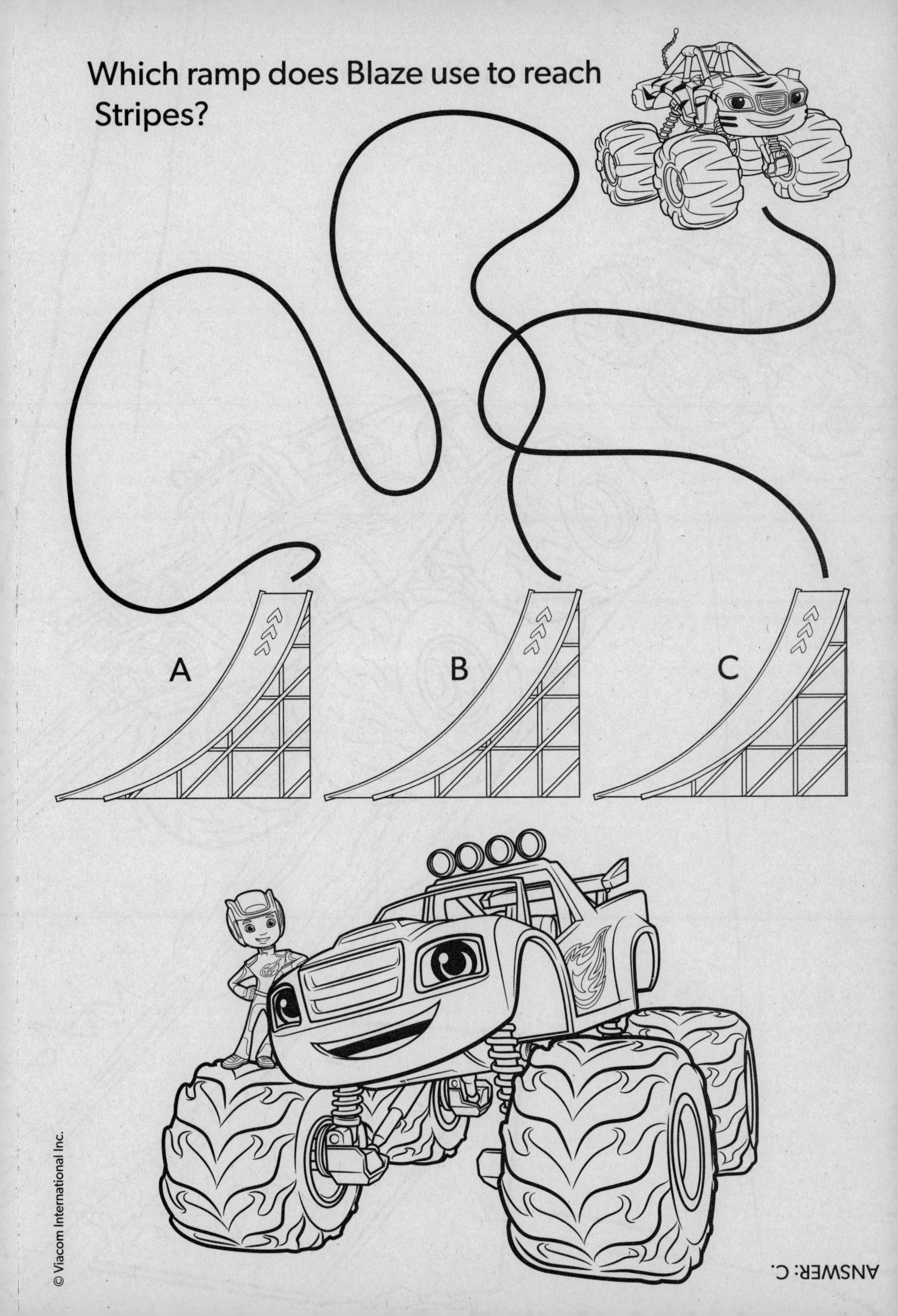

© Viacom International Inc.

ANSWER: C.

Blazing into action!

Blaze saves Stripes! High tire!

© Viacom International Inc.

Time to get back to the race. Let's *blaaaze*!

The Monster Machines find Darington. He's got trouble from some Grizzly Trucks!

© Viacom International Inc.

Find the Grizzly Truck who is different.

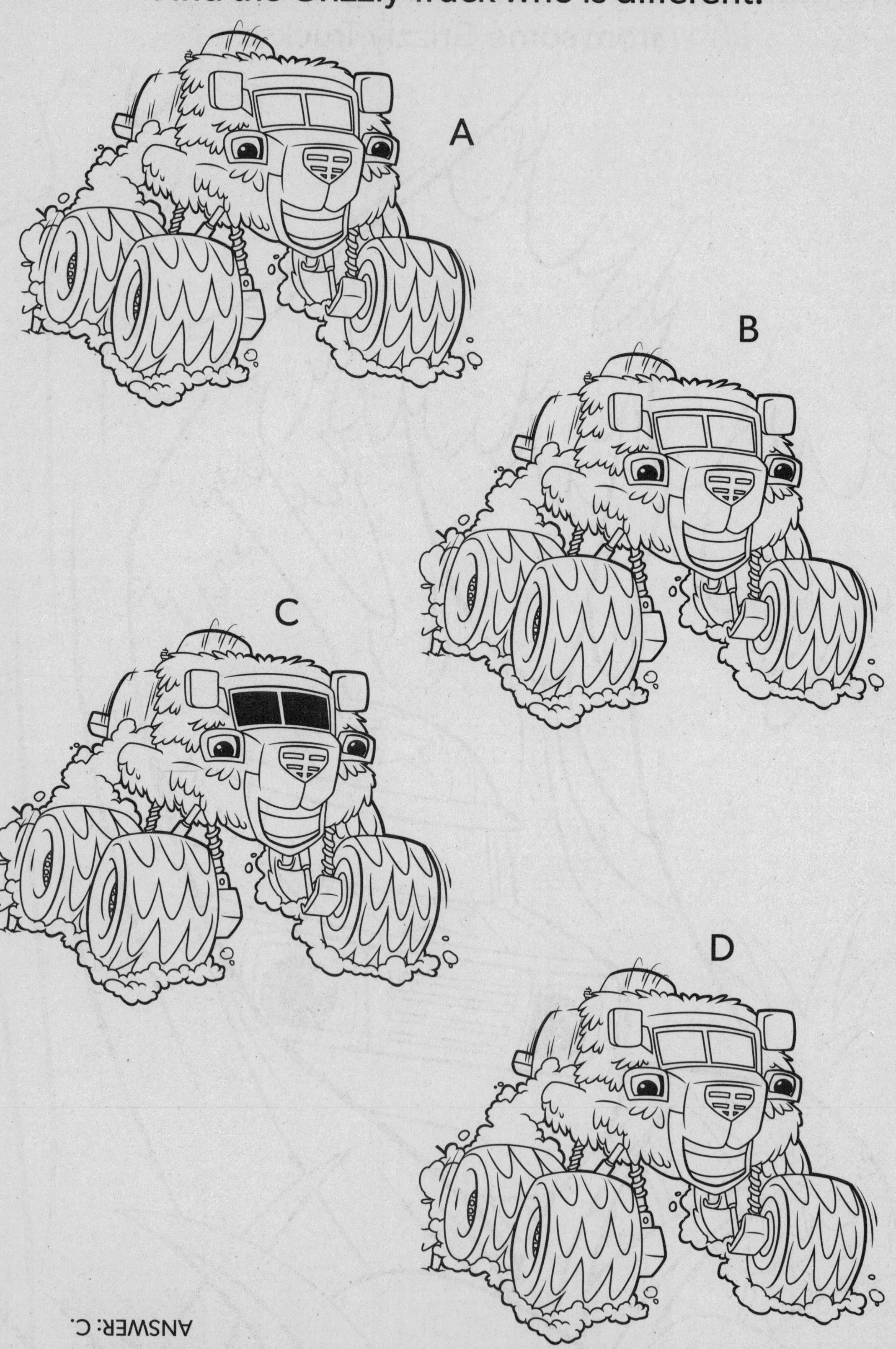

ANSWER: C.

The Monster Machines outrun the Grizzly Trucks and race back to the Monster Dome.

© Viacom International Inc.

Crusher comes up with another dirty trick.

Crusher's Mechanical Mudslinger flings mud balls at the Monster Machines!

© Viacom International Inc.

AJ helps attach a hose, a nozzle, and a spring-loaded arm to Blaze.

Blaze transforms into a water-spraying Sprinkler Monster Machine!

© Viacom International Inc.

Mud balls don't stand a chance against Blaze's super water-spraying sprinkler!

Blaze takes down the Mechanical Mudslinger!

© Viacom International Inc.

On their way back to the Monster Dome, Blaze and AJ see Zeg rolling down a mountain toward a cliff! Help them get to Zeg in time!

Saved!

© Viacom International Inc.

To get to the Monster Dome, the Monster Machines need to pass through a cave. But the entrance is too small.

ZEEEG!

© Viacom International Inc.

Inside the cave, the Monster Machines find Starla at the bottom of a hole.

Pulley power!

© Viacom International Inc.

The Monster Machines blaze back to the Monster Dome!
Match them to their close-ups.

ANSWER: A-3, B-2, C-4, D-1.

The Monster Machines make it back to the Monster Dome just in time for the race!

© Viacom International Inc.

Crusher cruises ahead.

© Viacom International Inc.

Stripes and Starla tumble into the tires!

Oil slick!

© Viacom International Inc.

Only Crusher and Blaze are left in the race.

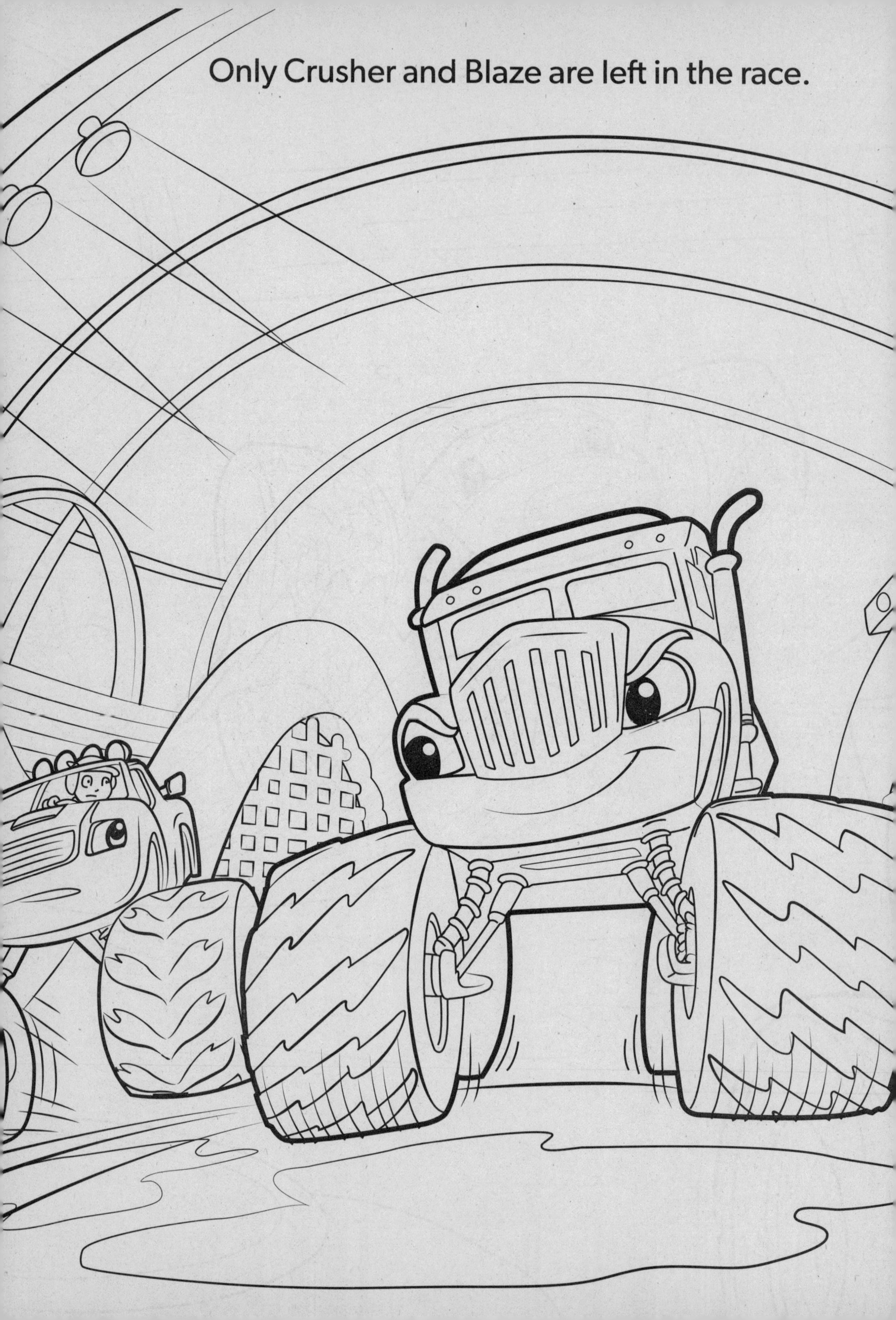

© Viacom International Inc.

Blaze the mighty Monster Machine wins the Monster Machine World Championship!